Stop, Thief!

O liver's eyes opened so wide that it looked like they might fall out of his head. What a shock it was to see the Dodger—his friend!—steal the wallet from the man's pocket, pass it over to Charley, and then run away. What a terrible thing to do!

For a moment, Oliver stood frozen with terror and shock. Then, not knowing what else to do, he took off after Charley and the Dodger.

At that very moment, the old gentleman put his hand in his pocket and realized he'd been robbed. Seeing Oliver running away, he pointed after him and shouted, "Stop, thief!"

READ ALL THE BOOKS
IN THE **wiSHBONe** *classics* SERIES:

Don Quixote

The Odyssey

Romeo and Juliet

Joan of Arc

Oliver Twist

*The Adventures of Robin Hood**

*Frankenstein**

The Strange Case of
*Dr. Jekyll and Mr. Hyde**

* coming soon

Wishbone Classics

OLIVER TWIST

by Charles Dickens

retold by Joanne Mattern

Interior illustrations by Ed Parker

Wishbone illustrations by
Kathryn Yingling

HarperPaperbacks

A Division of HarperCollins*Publishers*

HarperPaperbacks *A Division of* HarperCollins*Publishers*
10 East 53rd Street, New York, N.Y. 10022

Cover photographs by Carol Kaelson

A Creative Media Applications Production
Art Direction by Fabia Wargin Design
Project Management by Ellen Weiss
Edited by Matt Levine

First printing: July 1996

Printed in the United States of America

HarperPaperbacks and colophon are trademarks of
HarperCollins*Publishers*
WISHBONE is a trademark and service mark of
Big Feats! Entertainment

❖ 10 9 8 7 6 5 4 3 2 1

OLIVER TWIST

Introduction

All set to enter a world of action, adventure, drama, and laughs? Then come along with me, **Wishbone**. You may have seen me on my TV show. Often I am the main character and sometimes I am the sidekick, but I'm always right in the middle of a thrilling story. Now, I'm going to be your guide as we explore one of the world's greatest books — OLIVER TWIST. Together we'll meet a lot of interesting characters and discover places we've never been! I guarantee lots of surprises too! So find a nice comfy chair, and get ready to read with **Wishbone**.

Table of Contents

Charles Dickens

Imagine a life filled with tragedy and triumph, terrible poverty and overwhelming riches, loneliness and love. That's the sort of life the character of Oliver Twist had. It's also the life of Oliver's creator, Charles Dickens.

Charles Dickens was born on February 7, 1812. His father was a clerk in the British Navy. Although his father had a good job, he spent more money than he earned and was always deep in debt. As a result of this, Charles had to go to work in a shoe-polish factory when he was only twelve years old. Two weeks later, his parents and their four younger children were sent to debtors' prison (a place where people who owed money were forced to live until they could pay their debts). His home gone, Charles rented a room in a shabby part of town. He told no one the shameful news that his father had been sent to prison.

Charles's job in the shoe-polish factory was very dull. He had to cover each jar of polish with a label and tie it on with string. He did this twelve hours a day for just a tiny bit of money. But it was money his family desperately needed.

His miserable childhood made Charles determined to succeed. He studied in a law office and later became a court reporter. His formal schooling was limited, so he spent much of his free time reading books in the library and the British Museum.

When Charles was twenty years old, he began writing for a newspaper. His work allowed him to meet many different types of people, from criminals to rich members of Britain's upper class. Charles had a keen eye for observation, and many of these people he encountered would later turn up as characters in his novels.

In addition to writing for newspapers, Charles began writing books. His first book, *Sketches by Boz*, was published on his twenty-fourth birthday. What a nice present! He soon became one of the world's most popular writers. His books include such classics as *A Tale of Two Cities, David Copperfield,* and *Great Expectations*. Charles even went on speaking tours all over Europe and the United States to perform his work.

Although he became rich and successful, Charles never forgot the poverty and unhappiness of his childhood. Instead, he used the experiences of his own life to create the characters in his stories. Like Oliver Twist, Charles knew what it was like to be lonely, hungry, poor, and scared. Maybe that's why Oliver became one of Charles's best-known characters.

Here's another interesting fact about *Oliver Twist*. It was the first novel written in English that had a child as its hero. Most books at that time were about adults.

Charles used the characters in his novels, his gift for vivid description, and his biting sense of humor to make the public understand how harsh life was for poor people. By doing this, he hoped to change the unfair laws and attitudes that punished people just for being poor.

Charles Dickens died on June 8, 1870, while he was in the middle of writing *The Mystery of Edwin Drood*. The whole world mourned the loss of this great writer.

MAIN CHARACTERS

Oliver Twist — a young orphan

Mr. Gamfield — a chimney sweep

Mr. Sowerberry — an undertaker

Noah Claypole — an older boy who works for Mr. Sowerberry

Jack Dawkins (The Artful Dodger) — a boy in Fagin's gang

Fagin — the leader of a gang of criminals

Charley Bates — a boy in Fagin's gang

Mr. Brownlow — a generous man who takes care of Oliver

Mrs. Bedwin — Mr. Brownlow's housekeeper

Bill Sikes — Fagin's partner in crime

Nancy — Bill Sikes's girlfriend

Mr. Grimwig — Mr. Brownlow's friend

Edward Leeford (Monks) — a mysterious and sinister friend of Fagin's

Mrs. Maylie — a elderly woman who cares for Oliver

Rose Maylie — Mrs. Maylie's niece

efore you start reading Oliver's exciting story, it's a good idea to learn a little bit about where and when it takes place. *Oliver Twist* is set in the English city of London during the 1830s. That's over 160 years ago! Life was very different back then. For one thing, people didn't have cars—they got around by walking or riding in horse-drawn carriages. There were no telephones. If you wanted to tell somebody something, you had to write a letter or send a messenger.

In some parts of London, wealthy people lived in big houses with lots of servants. But not everyone in London was wealthy. Many folks didn't have enough to eat and lived in run-down houses in neighborhoods filled with crime.

In those days, many poor children didn't go to school. They had to work to help support their families. The jobs they had were exhausting and often very dangerous. Children worked long hours in factories, where they were sometimes injured or killed because the working conditions were not safe. Small boys often worked as chimney sweeps, squeezing into fireplaces and chimneys to clean them. Many boys suffocated or damaged their lungs doing this filthy job.

Many poor children belonged to gangs. Like Fagin's gang in *Oliver Twist*, these children roamed the streets, picking pockets, stealing, and committing other crimes. The streets were not very safe in those days!

The government did not make life any easier for poor people. In 1834, a law called the Poor Law forced able-bodied poor people to live in buildings called workhouses, where they were made to do difficult or dangerous jobs. Conditions in the workhouses were horrible, and many people died of disease and starvation. Charles Dickens began the story of *Oliver Twist* in a workhouse to show the public how awful life there really was.

Oliver Twist is one of Dickens's most famous books. People all over the world know about the orphan Oliver and his struggles to survive.

1
Born in a Workhouse

Our story begins at a very logical place—the beginning of Oliver's life. Our hero has a rough time of things from the start. Even at his birth, things don't go well for him.

The faint cry of a baby broke the early morning stillness of an English town. The cry came from a grim, gloomy place called the workhouse.

No one knew who the baby's mother was. She had been found lying in the street the night before and had been carried to the workhouse to have her baby. Poverty and illness had transformed the young woman into a pale, thin ghost of the pretty girl she once might have been.

The man in charge of the workhouse had a very practical system for naming the babies who were born there—he named them alphabetically. The last baby to be born at the workhouse had been named Swubble. Since the next letter of the alphabet was T, this baby was named Twist. His first name was to be Oliver.

At the sound of the baby's cry, his mother raised her head from the thin pillow on her bed. "Let me see the child," she asked weakly and stretched out her hands.

The doctor laid the baby in her arms. With tears streaming down her face, the mother kissed her child on the forehead and touched his cheek gently. Then she fell back on the bed, shuddered—and died.

Oliver cried as he was wrapped in a shabby yellow robe. Had he known that he was an orphan, with no friends or family to protect him, he might have cried even harder.

No one at the workhouse could care for the tiny new baby, so he was sent to another house run by an old woman named Mrs. Mann. Mrs. Mann was responsible for twenty or thirty children. The local government paid her an allowance to feed and clothe the children. Unfortunately, Mrs. Mann didn't see why the children needed good food and clothes, so she used most of the money to buy nice things for herself.

By the time Oliver was nine years old, he had grown into a pale, thin child who never had enough to eat and never had a kind word spoken to him. In fact, he spent his ninth birthday locked in the coal cellar with two other boys. All three boys had received a sound thrashing, merely because they had complained of being hungry! **It's a good thing no one punishes me when I'm hungry, or I'd be in trouble most of the time!**

Oliver's ninth birthday also brought the end of his time at Mrs. Mann's. He was now old enough to return to the workhouse and start earning his keep. And so, dressed in a hand-me-down shirt, pants, and cap, Oliver headed back to the place he was born.

Oliver wasn't sure whether he should be happy or sad to be leaving Mrs. Mann's house. He certainly wouldn't miss her cruel treatment and skimpy meals. But he was also anxious. What if the workhouse was a terrible place to live too? No one had ever treated Oliver kindly in his short life. He hoped things would be different now. But he knew better than to expect any kindness at all.

Poor Oliver! Will things be any better for him at the workhouse? Let's turn the page and see.

2
A Shocking Question

Oliver soon discovers that life at the workhouse is like life at Mrs. Mann's—no kindness and not enough food. And the building wasn't called a workhouse for nothing! Everyone was expected to work! Some of the residents were sent out to run machines in factories or pick crops on farms. Others did wealthy people's laundry—and there weren't any washing machines in those days to make that job easier! Children were expected to work just as hard as adults.

And no one got enough to eat. It was a pretty miserable existence. Oliver is about to try and improve things for himself and the other boys. Let's see what happens.

Mealtime at the workhouse was a grim event. All the boys filed into a stone hall. A large copper pot stood at one end. The boys lined up in front of the pot, each clutching a small bowl and spoon. Then the master of the house ladled out a bowlful of gruel for each boy. **Gruel is a thin mush made by boiling grains and water. You wouldn't feed it to a dog!**

After they had received their food, the boys sat at long tables and ate every drop of their skimpy meal. Then they sat staring at the copper pot as if they would like to gobble it down along with its watery contents.

After three months of eating nothing but small bowlfuls of gruel, Oliver and the other boys were practically starving. "If I don't get more to eat," announced a tall lad who was a bit of a bully, "I might just eat one of you boys in my sleep!" He stared at the younger boys with a wild, hungry look in his eyes.

"Someone has to ask for more food," another boy suggested, glancing nervously at the bully. "Let's cast lots and see who has to speak up."

So the boys took their chances, and Oliver ended up

the loser. "After supper this evening," the boys told him, "you must walk up to the master and ask for more."

Suppertime arrived. The boys took their places at the table and quickly gulped down their portions of gruel. Then they winked at Oliver, nudging him to step forward.

Oliver was frightened, but he was determined too. He knew all the other boys were counting on him. So he rose from his seat and walked up to the master, his bowl and spoon in his hand.

"Please, sir," Oliver asked in a soft voice. "I want some more."

The master turned pale with astonishment. "What?" he roared.

"Please, sir," Oliver repeated, louder this time. "I want some more!"

But Oliver didn't get more food. All he got for his courage was a whack on the head with the master's ladle. Then he was dragged out of the room. Word of his outrageous request was sent to the workhouse's board of directors. **The board of directors are the people who are in charge of a business. They make all the decisions.**

"Oliver Twist has asked for more?" the head of the board shouted. "Do you mean to tell me that after he had eaten his supper, he had the nerve to ask for more?"

"He did, sir," replied the master.

"That boy is no good," announced another member of the board. "Imagine asking for more when he had already eaten a perfectly good meal!"

"We must make an example of him so that no other boys get such ridiculous ideas," said the head of the board. "Lock him up in a dark room, where he'll have plenty of time to think about what he did. Meanwhile, we'll put a notice on the gate offering Oliver as an apprentice to anyone who will take him. That should keep him out of trouble—and get that ungrateful boy off our hands for good!" **An apprentice is someone who learns a trade by working for someone else. In those times, apprentices weren't paid for their work, and their bosses could do pretty much whatever they wanted with them.**

The board of directors posted a sign on the gate of the workhouse offering a reward of five pounds to anyone who would take Oliver as an apprentice. One morning, about a week after Oliver's request for more food, a chimney sweep named Mr. Gamfield was making his way in a cart past the workhouse. Mr. Gamfield was an unpleasant-looking man, whose ugly face seemed to indicate the man's cruel nature. At that moment, Mr. Gamfield was scowling terribly. He had a lot on his mind. His rent was due that day, and he did not have the money to pay it.

Just then, Mr. Gamfield saw the sign on the gate advertising Oliver Twist's service—and a five-pound reward. "That's just the amount of money I need! Whoa!" Mr. Gamfield shouted at the donkey that was pulling his cart. The donkey plodded on.

"Whoa, I said!" Mr. Gamfield yelled again, hitting the animal hard on the head. The donkey stumbled to a stop. Mr. Gamfield climbed down

There is something about this guy I don't like....

from the cart, gave the donkey another whack for good measure, and walked briskly up to the workhouse door.

"I've read your sign about this boy, Oliver Twist," Mr. Gamfield told the official who answered the door. "If you would like him to learn the *pleasant* trade of chimney sweeping, I would be happy to take him on as my apprentice."

"Come in and speak to the board of directors," the official said, leading Mr. Gamfield to the boardroom.

"Chimney sweeping, you say?" said Mr. Limbkins, one of the board members. "That's a nasty trade. Boys have been smothered in chimneys, haven't they?"

Mr. Gamfield pasted a phony smile across his grim features and laughed heartily. "Boys are very lazy and stubborn," he explained. "Sometimes they doze off inside the chimneys, you know, and you have to light a fire to get them moving."

"All right, then," the members of the board agreed after a brief discussion. "You may take the boy. Be sure to beat him now and then to keep him in line.

He shouldn't cost much for you to keep, for he hasn't been overfed since he was born."

Mr. Gamfield laughed at this good news. The owner of the workhouse was sent to fetch Oliver and bring him before the judge who would sign the papers, making the apprenticeship legal.

Oliver was nervous as he stepped before the judge. He looked around at all the strange faces in the room. When he saw Mr. Gamfield's scowling face, he began to tremble. Oliver could tell just by looking at him what a cruel man Mr. Gamfield was.

"So you want to be a chimney sweep, do you, boy?" asked the judge, a kind old gentleman wearing thick glasses.

Oliver was so frightened he could not speak. "Oh, yes, Your Honor," the owner of the workhouse spoke up quickly. "If we apprenticed him to any other trade, he'd run away."

"And you, Mr. Gamfield," said the judge, "do you swear you'll treat him well?"

"I said I would, and I will," Mr. Gamfield replied gruffly.

The judge nodded. Pushing his glasses up on his nose, he looked around for his pen to sign the document that would make Oliver Mr. Gamfield's apprentice.

Just then, the judge saw Oliver's terrified face. "My boy," the judge said, peering at the little boy. "Why do you look so frightened?"

Oliver was unable to answer. He burst into tears.

"Why are you crying, little one?" the judge asked kindly. "Don't be afraid."

Oliver looked from Mr. Gamfield's horrible face to the judge's kindly one. Then he threw himself on his knees and begged, "Please, Your Honor, don't send me away with him! You can beat me and starve me all you like. Just don't make me go with that dreadful man! He frightens me!"

"Why, you lying little—" the man from the workhouse began.

"Silence!" snapped the judge. "I refuse to agree to this apprenticeship. Take this poor boy back to the workhouse and treat him kindly. He seems to need it."

And so Oliver was spared a cruel fate at the hand of Mr. Gamfield. That very day, the sign advertising

Oliver's services and the reward for taking him went back up on the workhouse gate.

What a lucky break for Oliver! I wouldn't want a master like Mr. Gamfield holding my leash. Let's see what happens when Oliver's next potential master comes along.

3
Oliver Runs Away

It didn't take long before the workhouse had another offer for Oliver. An undertaker named Mr. Sowerberry took him on as his apprentice. Life at the Sowerberrys' was pretty grim. Mrs. Sowerberry was a grouchy woman who resented having another mouth to feed. She gave Oliver some leftover scraps of meat that the dog had refused to eat, and was alarmed when Oliver gobbled them down and looked for more. Worst of all, she made Oliver sleep among the empty coffins. Surrounded by the spooky coffins that would soon hold the bodies of the dead, Oliver barely dared to shut his eyes.

Daytimes were just as gloomy as the nights. Mr. Sowerberry was charmed by Oliver's sad, sweet face, and he soon began to bring him along to act as a hired mourner at funerals. Oliver attended many of these grim affairs. The children's funerals were the saddest of all.

Mr. Sowerberry had another apprentice, Noah Claypole. The older boy was mean and sneaky, and he bullied Oliver every chance he got. Oliver put up with all of this without complaining—until one day when Noah went too far.

Oliver and Noah were in the kitchen, eating their dinner. As they ate, Noah began to tease Oliver. He thought it would be great fun to make Oliver cry. But no matter how many names he called the boy or how many mean things he threatened to do to him, Noah could not bring Oliver to tears.

Then Noah thought of the perfect way to upset Oliver. "Tell me, how is your mother?" he asked.

"She's dead," Oliver said.

"Oh, what a pity," Noah said with a sneer. "You know, I heard your mother was a real bad woman."

Oliver looked up quickly. "What did you say?" he asked, his eyes flashing with anger.

"Only that your mother was bad. In fact, it's a lucky thing she died. Otherwise, she probably would have ended up in jail."

Hearing the cruel insult to his mother, quiet little Oliver exploded with rage. He jumped to his feet, knocked over the table and chair, and grabbed the surprised Noah by the throat. Then he shook the older boy so hard that his teeth rattled, and knocked Noah to the floor.

"Help!" Noah screamed. "He'll kill me! Help! Help!"

Mrs. Sowerberry and the maid ran into the room. "You wicked boy!" the maid yelled. She dragged Oliver away from Noah and began to hit him. Mrs. Sowerberry tried to hold Oliver down. Oliver struggled and shouted, fighting back as hard as he could. Finally the women dragged Oliver—who refused to go quietly—into the cellar and locked him in.

In the middle of all the excitement, Mr. Sowerberry came home. When he heard what had happened, he pulled Oliver out of the cellar and slapped him on the ear. "Aren't you a nice young fellow," he said. "Why were you fighting?"

Oliver scowled at Noah. "He called my mother names," he said.

"So what if he did?" Mrs. Sowerberry said. "She deserved what he said, and worse."

"She did not! That's a lie!" Oliver cried.

Mrs. Sowerberry burst into tears. Mr. Sowerberry

could not let his wife be called a liar, so he punished Oliver harshly, giving him a terrible beating.

Oliver was glad when he was finally sent to bed that night. Alone at last, he fell to his knees and wept bitterly for a long time. By the time his tears had stopped, Oliver had made a decision. He would no longer stay here among people who treated him cruelly. There had to be a better life for him somewhere in the world, and he was going to find it.

Quietly, carefully, Oliver crept to the door and slipped out of the room. Then he unbarred the front door and tiptoed into the street.

"I am going to seek my fortune far away from here," Oliver said, and set off down the road.

Now Oliver is on his own. What adventures lie in store for him?

4
The Artful Dodger

As Oliver walks along, he comes across a sign pointing the way to London, seventy miles away. Oliver has never been to London, but he knows it is a large place—so large that Mr. Sowerberry could never find him there! Oliver decides London is the perfect place to find a home, so that's where he heads.

The road to London was long and hard. Oliver walked miles and miles every day without anything to eat. He was so hungry that he even begged for food along the way, but most people wouldn't even look at him. Fortunately he met a kind-hearted man and an old lady who shared their bread and cheese with him. Otherwise Oliver might have starved to death before he ever got to London.

Despite his hardships, Oliver was determined to make it to the city. But lack of food wasn't the only problem he faced. At night he had to sleep in the fields, shivering in the cold air. His legs and feet ached from his long walk.

Seven days after he started his journey, Oliver limped into a little town called Barnet. Tired, sore, and hungry, Oliver sat down on a doorstep, not sure what to do next.

After a while, Oliver saw a boy staring at him. He was the strangest lad Oliver had ever seen. The boy was short and bow-legged, with sharp eyes that didn't miss a thing. Although he looked about the same age as Oliver, he walked with the confidence of a grown man. He wore a man's coat, which reached almost to his heels, and a top hat was perched lightly on his hair.

"Hello, my covey," the boy said, swaggering over to Oliver. "What's the row?" **What is this boy talking about? He's using slang, or common speech, from the time of Dickens to say hello and ask Oliver what's new.**

"I am very hungry and tired," Oliver told him. "I've been walking for seven days."

"Walking for seven days?" the young gentleman repeated. "Well, if you want food, I will see that you have it. I don't have much, but I'm happy to share. Come with me."

Oliver was so relieved to have someone show him kindness that he followed the strange boy into a shop, where he bought some ham and bread. Then they went into a public house to get something to drink.

A public house is a kind of restaurant.

Oliver gobbled down his meal with great enthusiasm. When he finished, the strange boy asked him, "So you're going to London?"

"Yes."

"Got any money or a place to stay?"

"No."

The boy whistled and shook his head.

"Do you live in London?" Oliver asked.

"Yes, I do—when I'm at home, that is," the boy answered pertly. "If you want a place to sleep tonight, I know a respectable old gentleman who will give you a place to stay for nothing."

This offer of free shelter was too good to pass up. Oliver quickly agreed.

"My name is Jack Dawkins," Oliver's new friend told him as they walked toward London. "But my friends call me the Artful Dodger."

The two boys didn't reach London until very late that night. As Oliver hurried along beside the Dodger, he couldn't help looking around him. The streets of London were narrow and filthy, and rough-looking people leaned out of doorways or staggered down the road.

Oliver was beginning to think coming to London hadn't been such a good idea if this was the sort of neighborhood he'd be living in. Before he could say anything, the Dodger suddenly grabbed his arm and pushed him through a doorway and into a house. Then he let out a piercing whistle.

"Now then," cried a voice from below.

"Plummy and slam!" the Dodger called back. Oliver realized that these strange words must be a password signaling that everything was all right.

A candle flickered at the end of the hallway and a man peeked out at them. "There's two of you," he said. "Who's with you, Dodger?"

"A new pal," the Dodger answered.

"Where did he come from?"

"Greenland," the Dodger joked. "Is Fagin upstairs?"

"Yes. Go on up."

Oliver stumbled up a flight of dark and broken stairs, struggling to keep up with the Dodger's quick steps. At the top, the Dodger threw open a door and pulled Oliver in after him.

Oliver could hardly believe his eyes. Standing over a frying pan filled with sausages was a very old, shriveled-up man. His ugly face was half-hidden by long, matted red hair, and he was dressed in a greasy flannel gown. The walls of the room were lined with simple beds, and a number of boys lay sleeping there.

Some other boys, eating at the table, grinned up at Oliver. So did the old man.

"Hello, Fagin," said the Dodger. "This is my friend, Oliver Twist."

Fagin bowed and shook Oliver's hand as if Oliver were the King of England. "I am pleased to meet you, young friend," the old man said. "Sit down and have some dinner with us."

Oliver ate and drank his fill. It was the first time in his life that he'd had enough to eat, and it was a wonderful feeling. After he'd finished, Oliver was so tired that he fell asleep right there at the table. He barely knew when Fagin put him to bed.

Oliver certainly has fallen into strange company, but these folks are treating him much better than anyone else ever has. Who is Fagin, and what is he up to? It doesn't take long for Oliver to find out.

5
Oliver's Education

It was late the next morning when Oliver awoke from a deep sleep. He lay quietly in bed, watching Fagin move around the room. The old man bent over and pulled a small box from a hole in the floor. His eyes sparkled as he raised the lid and peered inside. Then he pulled out a magnificent gold watch.

Oliver could hardly believe his eyes. He had never seen anything so beautiful in his life. As he watched secretly, Fagin pulled more watches out of the box. Each one was as beautiful as the first. Then came rings, pins, bracelets, and other pieces of jewelry.

Fagin smiled as he handled each gold piece. "What beautiful treasures," he whispered. Then he looked up—and caught Oliver staring at him.

The lid of the box slammed shut with a bang. "What are you staring at me for?" Fagin demanded, leaping to his feet. "What did you see?"

"N-nothing, sir," Oliver stammered. "I just woke up."

The old man bent menacingly over the frightened boy. "You're sure you saw nothing?" he asked.

"Upon my word, sir. I'm sorry if I disturbed you."

"All right, then." Fagin patted the box. "These are just some trinkets that belong to me. It's nothing to concern you."

"Of course not," Oliver agreed. "May I get up now?"

"Yes. There's a basin in the corner. Go wash up."

Oliver did as Fagin told him. When he turned around again, the box was gone.

A few minutes later, the Artful Dodger came into the room. With him was another boy, Charley Bates. Charley was a cheerful lad, always smiling and laughing, even if nothing was funny.

The boys sat down to breakfast together. "Have you been working hard this morning?" Fagin asked the Dodger and Charley.

"Hard as nails," the Artful Dodger replied. "See, I've found a couple of wallets." He placed two leather wallets, jingling with coins, on the table.

"And I have some wipes," Charley said. He

dropped a pile of crisp white handkerchiefs on the table.

"Very good, very good!" Fagin said. "Oliver, you'd like to find some treasures too, wouldn't you?"

"I'd like to very much," said Oliver, who was eager to please this kind old gentleman. Charley Bates laughed, though Oliver didn't think he'd said anything funny.

When breakfast was cleared away, the Dodger and Charley began to play a strange game. Fagin slipped a watch in one pocket, a handkerchief in another, and a wallet in a third. Then he began to walk up and down the room as if he were strolling down the main street of town.

The Artful Dodger and Charley followed the old man closely. Sometimes the Dodger would bump into Fagin, or step on his toes, while Charley stumbled against him from behind. Quick as a wink, the boys would pull Fagin's watch, wallet, and handkerchief from his pockets. If Fagin felt their hands in his pockets he would call out, and the game would begin again.

While Fagin and the boys played their strange

game, several young women stopped in to say hello and watch the fun. One of them, named Nancy, smiled when she was introduced to Oliver and talked to him for a little while. She was sloppily dressed and her hair needed a good combing, but she had a kind face and a delightful smile. Oliver thought she was very nice, and he was sorry when she left.

"Here, Oliver, you give it a try," Fagin said after a while. Oliver was pleased to join in the merry game. He crept behind Fagin and drew the old man's handkerchief out of his pocket as quickly and carefully as he could.

"Well done!" Fagin cried. "What a clever boy! You'll soon be out working with the Dodger and Charley. What a team you boys will be! But first, come here, Oliver. There's something else I'd like to teach you."

The old man picked up one of the handkerchiefs that Charley had brought him and showed it to Oliver. "See these letters sewn into the cloth?" Fagin asked, pointing at an embroidered monogram. **A monogram is a person's initials.** "See if you can pick them out with this needle without tearing the cloth."

Oliver did as he was told. Fagin was pleased with the neat job he did.

And so, for the next several days, Oliver sat in Fagin's room picking out the letters from handkerchiefs. There seemed to be a never-ending supply, as the boys brought more home every day. But Oliver didn't wonder where all the handkerchiefs came from, or why they had people's initials sewn into them. He was just happy to be part of this friendly group.

That game the boys were playing seems pretty odd, doesn't it? It looks like picking pockets to me, and that means stealing! And where did Fagin get all that gold? There's something funny going on here, but Oliver is too innocent to suspect anything. Oliver's innocence is about to get him into big trouble!

6
Stop, Thief!

A few days later, Fagin gives Oliver permission to go out with Charley and the Dodger. The three boys head toward a busy shopping district. It doesn't take long for Oliver to see his new friends at work.

The three boys ambled along the crowded street, looking this way and that. Oliver was beginning to wonder what they were supposed to be doing when the Artful Dodger stopped short and ducked into a doorway.

"What's the matter?" Oliver asked.

"Be quiet!" the Dodger whispered. "Do you see that old cove standing in front of the book-stall?" Oliver nodded. "He'll do," the Dodger said.

"A perfect choice," Charley added, smothering a giggle.

Oliver looked from one to the other in complete confusion. Before he could ask what was going on, the

Dodger and Charley crept up behind the old gentleman. Oliver walked a few steps behind them.

The man's name was Mr. Brownlow. He was a very respectable looking fellow, with a powdered wig and gold spectacles. He was elegantly dressed in a coat with a black velvet collar, and he carried a slim bamboo cane under one arm. He had just picked up a book from an outdoor display and was reading it intently.

As Oliver watched in horror, the Dodger plunged his hand into Mr. Brownlow's pocket and pulled out a wallet. He handed it to Charley, and the two boys ran around the corner.

Instantly, Oliver understood the meaning of Fagin's box full of jewels and the pocket-picking game. His friends were thieves! **I had a feeling they were up to no good!**

Oliver's eyes opened so wide that it looked like they might fall out of his head. What a shock it was to see the Dodger—his friend!—steal the wallet from the man's pocket, pass it over to Charley, and then run away. What a terrible thing to do!

For a moment, Oliver stood frozen with terror and shock. Then, not knowing what else to do, he took off after Charley and the Dodger.

At that very moment, the old gentleman put his hand in his pocket and realized he'd been robbed. Seeing Oliver running away, he pointed after him and shouted, "Stop, thief!" Then he ran after the boy.

Mr. Brownlow was not the only person to give chase. Many people in the crowd heard the gentleman and followed him, all yelling for Oliver to stop. The Artful Dodger and Charley joined in, shouting "Stop, thief!" louder than anyone.

It didn't take long for the crowd to overcome

poor Oliver and knock him down. Oliver lay on the ground, covered with mud and dust, blood trickling from his mouth where someone had hit him. He looked fearfully around the circle of faces staring down at him and saw only anger there.

Mr. Brownlow finally caught up with the crowd and bent over the frightened boy to get a good look at him. Something about Oliver seemed strangely familiar. He was just about to ask Oliver a question when a policeman pushed his way through the crowd and grabbed Oliver by the collar.

"You say this boy robbed you?" the officer asked.

"Yes," Mr. Brownlow replied faintly. "At least I *think* it was him."

"Come along," the policeman said roughly, dragging Oliver down the street.

"It wasn't me, sir. Honest," Oliver said desperately. "It was two

Helllooo! Start flipping the book pages and check out the action . . . . Woo-cha!

other boys. I'm not a thief!" But the policeman said nothing. He just pushed Oliver along.

"Don't hurt him!" called Mr. Brownlow, hurrying to keep up.

Oliver and Mr. Brownlow were brought immediately before a judge. "Are you the man who was robbed?" a court officer asked Mr. Brownlow.

"Yes, but I am not sure this boy actually took the wallet. I would rather not press charges."

"It's too late now," the officer said with a shrug. "Here's the judge."

As the judge entered the courtroom, Mr. Brownlow stared at Oliver again. The boy looked so frightened and sad that it almost broke the old gentleman's tender heart. There was something very familiar about Oliver's face, yet Mr. Brownlow was sure he'd never met the boy before.

The police officer who had captured Oliver explained what had happened. Then it was Mr. Brownlow's turn. He explained how he'd been standing in front of the bookstore when his pocket was picked. "I saw this boy running away," he said, gesturing at Oliver, "and I gave chase. But now I am not sure he was the thief. Please take that into consideration, Your Honor."

"Certainly," the judge muttered impatiently. He glared at Oliver, who was swaying on his feet.

"I think the boy is ill, Your Honor," the police officer said, looking concerned.

"Oh, he's probably just faking it to get our sympathy," the judge scoffed.

Suddenly poor Oliver fainted in a heap on the floor. "Your fainting act won't work with me'" said the judge. "I pronounce the boy guilty as charged and sentence him to three months' hard labor!"

Oh, no! Oliver is really in big trouble now. How will he ever get out of this?

7
A Mysterious Resemblance

Oliver's treatment at the hands of the law seems pretty rough and unfair, don't you think? Well, that's the way the court system worked in those days. A person who was accused of a crime didn't have the right to a lawyer or a jury trial as we do today. The accused couldn't even speak up in his or her own defense! And the punishments were much more severe than today's courts hand out. In fact, people could be executed for even minor crimes! So three months of hard labor for a little boy accused of stealing wasn't anything unusual for that time and place.

Two court officers stepped forward to drag the unconscious Oliver out of the courtroom. Just then, a man rushed into the room. "Stop! Stop!" he shouted.

"Who are you?" the judge roared. "How dare you disturb my courtroom!"

"You must listen to me," the man demanded. "I am the owner of the book-stall. I have something important to say."

"Oh, all right," the judge said. "What is it?"

"I saw three boys—the prisoner and two others—standing near my stall. It was the other boys who robbed Mr. Brownlow. The prisoner watched, and I could tell he was shocked by the whole thing. He had no part in the robbery, none at all."

"Well, then," the judge grumbled. "Case dismissed. Now, everyone clear the courtroom!"

Everyone hurried outside. Someone laid Oliver on the ground and poured water over his head in an effort to revive him.

"The poor boy!" Mr. Brownlow exclaimed. He signaled a passing carriage to stop and carefully put Oliver inside. Then he climbed in and gave directions to his house. **In the old days, horse-drawn carriages were like our modern taxicabs.**

The carriage made its way to a fine part of town called Pentonville. When they reached his house, Mr.

Brownlow hurried inside and ordered his housekeeper, Mrs. Bedwin, to prepare the guest room and put the boy to bed. "I want to give that poor boy the best of care to make up for the trouble he went through today," the gentleman promised. "He certainly needs someone to take care of him!"

It was many days before Oliver regained his strength. Mr. Brownlow and Mrs. Bedwin fussed over him constantly. Oliver had never known such kindness.

After a while, Oliver was well enough to get out of bed and sit downstairs by the fireplace in the housekeeper's room. Mrs. Bedwin was charmed by the little boy and delighted in seeing that he was comfortable and had everything he wanted. Oliver soon came to love Mrs. Bedwin because of her kind treatment of him. The two quickly grew close and devoted to each other.

One day as Mrs. Bedwin fixed him some soup, Oliver looked around the room, marveling at all the pretty things there.

"What a lovely house this is," Oliver said. "I've never seen anything so fine. There are so many beautiful paintings hanging on the wall!"

"Do you like paintings?" Mrs. Bedwin asked.

"I don't know. I have seen so few. But I do like that picture," Oliver said, pointing to a portrait of a young woman. "What a kind, pretty face she has. Who is it?"

"I don't know," Mrs. Bedwin said. "No one you or I know, I suppose."

Just then, Mr. Brownlow came into the room. He nodded hello to Oliver, then looked up at the painting that had so captured the boy's attention.

"Mrs. Bedwin, look at that!" the old gentleman shouted in surprise. He pointed from Oliver's face to the face in the portrait. "The resemblance is unbelievable!"

Indeed, Oliver's face was exactly like the woman's. The eyes, the nose, the mouth, even the expression on both faces—every feature was the same.

Now here's an interesting development. Who is the woman in the painting, and why does Oliver look so much like her? There's more to this puzzle than meets the eye!

8
Find Oliver!

What's been happening at Fagin's hideout while Oliver is staying at Mr. Brownlow's? Well, Fagin is furious when the Artful Dodger and Charley Bates tell him that Oliver was arrested. The old man has some pretty nasty plans up his sleeve—plans that mean bad news for Oliver!

"What do you mean Oliver was arrested?" Fagin shouted at the Artful Dodger. He grabbed a pot and flung it at the Dodger and Charley. The boys ducked, and the pot found another target.

"Hey, what did you do that for?" demanded a man just entering the doorway. He rubbed his head and glared at Fagin angrily.

"Sorry, Bill," Fagin apologized nervously to his partner.

Bill Sikes was a heavily built fellow of about

thirty-five. He was dressed in a shabby black jacket and dirty pants, and a stained kerchief was tied around his neck. Several days' growth of beard darkened his scowling face, and there was a bruise next to one of his eyes.

Sikes turned back to the open door. "Come in, you hear?" he growled. A white shaggy dog with a scratched, torn face slunk slowly into the room.

"Get in here, Bull's-eye," Sikes muttered to his dog. "Lie down!" The command was accompanied by a kick which sent the animal across the room. Bull's-eye seemed used to this sort of treatment, though. He curled himself into a ball and lay quietly, looking around the room.

> Hey! Watch how you treat that dog, pal!

"Give me something to drink," Sikes demanded of Fagin. "And don't poison it!" He trusted Fagin about as much as Fagin trusted him—which was not much.

Fagin hurried to do what Sikes asked. Although

he and Sikes worked together, Fagin was scared of this violent man. He knew Sikes was capable of anything.

As Sikes gulped down his drink, Fagin told him about Oliver's arrest. "I'm afraid the boy will talk too much and get us into trouble," he said. "You know we all work together here. Oliver might not keep our secrets as well as he should."

"You're probably right," Sikes agreed, scowling. "Someone will have to go to the police station and find out what happened to the boy."

"Not me!" Charley Bates cried, laughing nervously.

"Not me!" the Artful Dodger echoed.

"Well, *I* certainly can't go near a police station," Fagin said.

"Neither can I," Sikes added. "Who can we send?"

Just then, Sikes's girlfriend, Nancy, came into the room. "Nancy, my dear!" Fagin said when he saw her. "How would you like to do me a favor?"

"I'm not talking to the police!" Nancy said when Fagin told her what needed to be done.

"Nancy, my girl, you're just the one to do it,"

Sikes told her. "No one there knows you—at least not as well as they know us."

"I said I won't go," Nancy insisted.

"And I said you will," Sikes said, his voice harsh and threatening.

Sikes threatened Nancy until the young woman finally agreed to go. She tucked her hair under a hat and picked up a covered basket to carry. Now that she looked a bit more respectable, she was ready to face the police.

When she reached the station, Nancy walked up to a police officer and burst into tears. "Oh, my poor brother!" she wailed. "What has become of the child? Oh, sir, you must help me find him!" **Her brother? What a good actress this Nancy is!**

"There, there, don't cry, my dear," said the policeman kindly. "Tell me who you're looking for and I'll see what I can do."

"My little brother," Nancy sobbed. "I just heard he was arrested for picking a gentleman's pocket. But he's a good boy, honest he is! Please don't send him to jail!"

"Oh, that boy," the policeman said. "We haven't got him here. The old gentleman took him away."

"What old gentleman?" Nancy shrieked, bursting into fresh sobs.

The policeman quickly told Nancy all that had happened in court that morning. "I heard the gentleman say he lived in Pentonville, but I don't know the exact address," he finished.

"Oh, thank you, sir," Nancy said. "You've been so kind." Then she hurried down the street. But she did not head toward Pentonville. Instead, she made her way back to Fagin's quarters.

"We must know exactly where he is," Fagin said when Nancy told them what the policeman had said. He pointed at the boys sitting around the room. "Charley, Dodger, all of you, there is just one thing I want you to do. Find Oliver and bring him back to me—any way you can!"

Why can't Fagin leave Oliver alone? The boy is certainly better off staying with Mr. Brownlow. But Fagin has some kind of plan for Oliver, and for some reason the boy is very important to him. Oliver better watch out!

9

A Test of Honesty

Oliver doesn't know that Fagin and his gang are plotting against him. In fact, Oliver isn't thinking about Fagin at all—he's just enjoying his new life at Mr. Brownlow's. But something is about to happen that will change everything.

Oliver had never known such a life as he had at Mr. Brownlow's. Everything was so quiet and pleasant there, and everyone was so kind to him. It was such a change from the cruel, harsh life he'd lived before that Oliver could hardly believe his good fortune. He'd never imagined he could live such a comfortable, happy life!

Mr. Brownlow had a new suit of clothes made for Oliver to wear. Oliver couldn't wait to get rid of his old clothes. He gave them to a servant to sell to the rag merchant and was very glad to think that he'd never have to wear those clothes again. **People used to buy and sell old clothes to use as rags.**

One day, as Oliver sat talking to Mrs. Bedwin, Mr. Brownlow sent a message downstairs that he would like to speak to Oliver in his study.

"Bless us," Mrs. Bedwin exclaimed. "Quick, Oliver, run and wash your hands, and let me comb your hair for you." She fluttered nervously around the boy. "If only I'd known Mr. Brownlow was going to ask for you, I would have put a clean shirt on you and made you look as smart as sixpence!"

At last, Mrs. Bedwin decided that Oliver looked presentable and took him upstairs. Oliver had never been in Mr. Brownlow's study before. The room was filled with books. "I have never seen so many books," Oliver said, looking about him in wonder.

"You shall read them someday, if you like," Mr. Brownlow said. "Now, I want to speak to you plainly about some important matters."

"Oh, please, don't tell me you are going to send me away!" Oliver cried in alarm. "Don't turn me out to wander the streets again. Please let me stay here. I could be a servant, or—"

"My dear boy," Mr. Brownlow said, "don't worry! I will never abandon you—unless you give me reason to."

"I never will," Oliver promised.

"Good. Now then, I want to hear your story. Tell me where you come from and how you got into the bad company in which I found you."

Oliver was just about to tell Mr. Brownlow his tale when there was a knock on the door. A stout old gentleman entered the room, walking with the help of a cane. He was elegantly dressed in a blue jacket and a frilled shirt, and a long steel watch chain dangled from his belt. Despite his elegant appearance, Oliver thought he was very strange-looking. The man turned his head to one side whenever he spoke, which made him look like a parrot.

"Hello," Mr. Brownlow said. "Oliver, this is my good friend, Mr. Grimwig. Mr. Grimwig, this is young Oliver, whom I was telling you about."

Mr. Grimwig stamped his cane on the floor and peered at Oliver. "So this is the boy," he said. "Hello, boy."

"Hello, sir," Oliver said timidly.

Mr. Grimwig pulled Mr. Brownlow aside and spoke to him quietly so Oliver wouldn't hear. "I can't believe you have taken this boy into your house when you know nothing about him. Where does he come from? Is he from a good family or a bad one? I tell you, you'd better count your money at night and make sure none is missing!"

"You mustn't speak that way," Mr. Brownlow said. "Oliver is a good boy, and he hasn't caused us a bit of trouble since he's been here. Come, let's have our tea."

As Oliver and the gentlemen were enjoying their meal, Mrs. Bedwin hurried in with a package of books. "The boy from the bookstore just brought these," she said.

Tea isn't just a hot drink in England. It's a whole meal, including little sandwiches, cookies, and pastries—and tea, of course—served late in the afternoon. An extra meal every day sure sounds good to me!

"Oh, I have some books for him to take back," Mr. Brownlow said.

"The boy's already left," Mrs. Bedwin said.

"Oh, dear. I really wanted those books to go back to the store today."

"Why don't you send Oliver with them?" Mr. Grimwig said with a mocking smile. "I'm sure he'll deliver them safely." His voice was heavy with sarcasm. **Sarcasm is when you say one thing, but you mean the exact opposite. Mr. Grimwig said that Oliver**

would deliver the books safely, but he really meant that Oliver wouldn't.

"Yes, do let me take them," Oliver agreed. "I'll run all the way."

"All right," Mr. Brownlow said, glancing at Mr. Grimwig. He gave Oliver the books and a five-pound note to pay his bill.

"I'll be back in ten minutes," Oliver promised and hurried outside.

"You don't really expect him to come back, do you?" Mr. Grimwig asked.

"Of course I do," Mr. Brownlow replied. "Why shouldn't he?"

"He has a new suit of clothes on his back, a set of valuable books under his arm, and a five-pound note in his pocket," Mr. Grimwig reminded him. "He'll go straight back to his thieving friends and laugh at you. Why, if that boy ever returns to this house, I'll eat my hat!"

"We shall see."

The two friends sat in silence, waiting for Oliver to return. The minutes passed, and then the hours. The room grew so dark that the two men could no longer see the numbers on the clock. Oliver did not come home.

What has happened to Oliver? You don't think he's run away with Mr. Brownlow's money, do you? Something terrible must have happened to him. Let's turn the page and find out what's going on.

10
Kidnapped!

Oliver hurried through the streets. He was happy to be running an errand for Mr. Brownlow and determined to return home as quickly as possible to prove that he was a reliable and trustworthy boy.

Oliver didn't know his way around London very well, and he accidentally turned down the wrong street. Halfway down, he realized his mistake. "I am still heading in the right direction," Oliver said to himself. "I don't want to waste time turning around and going back, and I'm sure the bookstore is close by." So he continued on his way.

Suddenly, a young woman jumped in front of him and flung her arms around his neck. "My dear brother!" she cried. It was Nancy.

"What are you talking about?" Oliver said, struggling in her arms.

"Thank goodness I've found him," Nancy went on loudly. "My dear brother, Oliver! How worried we've all been since you ran away! Come home with me."

"But I'm not—" Oliver began.

"Here, boy, go home with your sister," said a passerby who had heard Nancy's words. "You should be ashamed for worrying your family."

"That's right," shouted another man. "Go on home!"

The whole crowd began to shout at Oliver as Nancy hurried him along the street. Then Bill Sikes stepped out of a doorway and grabbed Oliver's other arm. There was no escape.

Sikes's dog, Bull's-eye, trotted along beside them. "If you shout or try to get away, Bull's-eye will tear your throat out," Sikes warned Oliver. Bull's-eye growled and licked his lips, staring at the terrified boy.

Nancy and Sikes dragged Oliver through the twisting streets. At last they came to a narrow street crowded with run-down shops and houses. Sikes grabbed Oliver by the collar, dragged him into one of the houses, and pushed him down the steps into a small room. There sat Fagin, the Artful Dodger, and Charley Bates.

"Well, look who's come back to us at last," Fagin said.

"And he's dressed so nicely too," Charley Bates said. "I can hardly look at him! What a jolly game!" The boy burst into a fit of laughter at Oliver's elegant appearance.

"Yes, just look at these togs, Fagin," the Artful Dodger added. "He's carrying books too. What a gentleman!"

"Oliver, we'll just have to give you some other clothes to wear," Fagin said. "That suit is much too fine to wear every day." He shoved a bundle of cloth into Oliver's arms. Oliver recognized the old clothes he had given away. "I bought them from the rag merchant," Fagin said as Oliver stared in disbelief at his old clothes. "It was our first clue to where you were."

The Artful Dodger stepped forward and deftly pulled the five-pound note from Oliver's pocket. "I'll take that," Sikes said, snatching the bill away. "It will be my pay for running all over London looking for this worthless boy. You can keep the books, Fagin."

"Stop!" Oliver shouted. "The money and the books belong to the old gentleman who took me in.

He'll think I've stolen them if you don't give them back."

"That's right, Oliver," Fagin said. "He *will* think you've stolen them, and he won't want anything more to do with you. Too bad. You've been a very naughty boy, Oliver, running away from us when we've been so kind to you. Is that the thanks we get for caring for you when you didn't know a soul here in London? Now go to bed. You won't be going outside for many a day—not until you prove we can trust you."

Oliver had no choice but to do as Fagin told him. *I can hardly believe this is happening to me*, he thought in despair. *All I want is to escape this den of thieves and return to Mr. Brownlow! But I have no idea how to do that. Mr. Brownlow probably won't even take me back if he thinks I am a thief.* The horror of the situation was like a weight on Oliver's thin shoulders. He was trapped.

Poor Oliver! Now he's back in Fagin's clutches, just when he thought he was safe at Mr. Brownlow's! What's going to happen to Oliver next?

11
Dangerous Plans

Fagin kept Oliver locked up for a long time, and he didn't let him see or speak to anyone outside the gang. Imagine how you'd feel if you weren't allowed to talk to anybody or even leave the house. You'd feel pretty trapped, just like I would if I were kept in a fenced-in yard all day. In time, you might not even remember what your life used to be like before you were locked up. That's what happened to Oliver—he began to forget what living at Mr. Brownlow's was like. Then Fagin decided it was time for Oliver to earn his keep, so he had a talk with Bill Sikes.

It was a chilly, damp, windy night when Fagin made his way through the muddy streets. A black mist hung over the town, making everything feel clammy and cold.

Fagin made his stealthy way through the streets until he came to the narrow house where Sikes was living. He crept inside and tapped on the door of one of the rooms.

"Who's there?" a rough voice shouted.

"It's only me, Bill," Fagin said, slipping into the room.

Bill Sikes and Nancy were seated near the fire, trying to keep warm. Nancy gestured for Fagin to join them near the blaze.

"It's awfully cold out," Fagin said, rubbing his hands together over the fire.

"It must be if the cold can find a way through *your* heart," Sikes snapped, unable to resist a dig at his partner's hard-hearted ways. "It's about time you got here. I need to talk business with you."

"Is this about the house in Chertsey?" Fagin asked.

"That's right. That house is loaded with riches just waiting for the likes of me to take them away."

"What are you waiting for then?" Fagin asked.

"I've been spying around there, and the place is locked up tighter than tight. But there is one way in."

"What's that?"

"I'm not telling *you*," Sikes said with a sneer. "How do I know you won't do the job yourself and keep all the goods? No, I'll take care of everything. But I need a boy to go with me."

"A small boy who would fit through a small window," Fagin guessed with a crafty smile.

"Never mind. Just tell me which of your lads would be good for the job."

"How about Oliver?" Fagin suggested. "I've been training him well the last few weeks, and it's time he began to work for his bread."

"Oh, why Oliver?" Nancy asked. "Isn't there another boy?"

"He is just the size I want—small and thin," Sikes said thoughtfully.

"And he'll do anything you want," Fagin said, "especially if you frighten him enough. It'll be perfect, Bill. Once Oliver does a job for us, he'll be a thief for life. If he gives us any trouble in the future, we can hold this crime against him, and he'll be afraid to run to the police or anyone else."

"I'll want him tomorrow night," said Sikes. "Nancy, you'll fetch him for me."

"All right," the girl agreed, although she was worried. She genuinely liked Oliver—he was such a sweet, harmless boy. She didn't like the idea of his getting involved with thieves like Sikes and Fagin. Nancy wanted a better life for Oliver.

• • • • • •

When Oliver awoke in the morning, he was surprised to find a new pair of sturdy shoes next to his bed. He was pleased with this discovery. *Perhaps they mean to let me go back to Mr. Brownlow,* he thought.

But Oliver's hopes were dashed as soon as he sat down to breakfast with Fagin. "Oliver, my boy," the old man said as he toasted a piece of bread over the fire, "you'll be going to Bill Sikes's house tonight."

"T-to stay?" Oliver stammered fearfully.

"No, no," Fagin reassured him. "I wouldn't want to lose you. You'll just be helping him with something. Bill will tell you all about it. I'll say this much—you must do whatever Bill tells you to do. He's a rough one, and he won't think twice about hurting you if you cross him."

Fagin would tell Oliver nothing else. He left the room, giving the boy a book to read while he waited for Nancy to come.

Oliver flipped through the pages. He realized this book was a history of the lives of notorious criminals. Oliver's blood ran cold as he read about dreadful murders committed in the dark of night, of bodies hidden in wells or shallow graves along the road. The descriptions were so real and vivid that the pages of the book seemed to turn red with blood.

Terrified, Oliver slammed the book shut and shoved it away from him. He fell to his knees and began to pray. "Spare me from such horrible deeds," he begged. "I would rather die than be involved in such horrible crimes!"

After a while, Oliver grew calmer, but he stayed on his knees to offer up one last prayer. "If anyone can help a poor, outcast boy escape, please help me!"

Oliver had just finished his prayer when Nancy slipped into the room. She was pale and trembling. "God forgive me," she murmured as she took his hand.

"What's wrong?" Oliver asked.

"Nothing," Nancy said, forcing herself to smile. "Come along. I'm to bring you to Bill."

"What for?" Oliver asked.

"Oh, for no harm," Nancy said quickly.

"I don't believe that," Oliver answered.

"Have it your way," Nancy said. "For no good then." She bent close to Oliver. "Listen," she whispered. "I want to help you, but there's nothing I can do now. If you are ever to escape from here, this is not the time. You must come quietly with me. I promise I won't hurt you. That is why I agreed to fetch you—because I knew that others who might have brought you to Bill would not have been gentle about it! Now give me your hand and let's go!"

Oliver did as Nancy told him. They walked quickly and quietly through the streets until they came to Sikes's house.

"Bill!" Nancy called, pushing Oliver forward. "Here's the boy."

"Did he come quietly?" Sikes asked.

"Quiet as a lamb," Nancy said.

"Good. Now listen here, young'un," Sikes said. "If you speak a word or don't do as I say, I'll kill you. Don't think I won't! Understand?"

"Y-yes," Oliver stammered, shaking with fear. He looked at Nancy, hoping she could do something to help him, but the girl turned her face away.

I sure wouldn't want Bill Sikes holding my leash! What's going to happen to Oliver now? I have the feeling it won't be good!

12
A Job Gone Wrong

Oliver and Sikes spent most of the next day walking through London. Oliver was too afraid to ask Sikes where they were heading or what he planned to do there. The only time Sikes spoke to Oliver was to shout at him. "Don't lag behind, lazy-legs," the man snarled, grabbing Oliver's wrist and jerking him through the streets.

It was very late the next night when Oliver and Sikes arrived at a small town called Chertsey, on the outskirts of London. Oliver was so tired he could barely walk, but an angry look from Sikes was enough to force him to stumble along without complaining.

It was so late that the streets of the town were completely deserted. A few lights burned in the windows of the houses, and the occasional barking of a dog broke the stillness, but Oliver and Sikes passed no other person on the road.

Finally they turned off the road and came upon a house behind a high wall. "Over you go," Sikes said, giving Oliver a rough shove to the top of the wall. Oliver jumped down to the other side, and Sikes landed softly beside him. They crept through the darkness toward the house.

Oliver suddenly understood that Sikes meant for them to break into this house and rob it. Horrified, he fell to his knees in the grass. "Please, Mr. Sikes," he begged. "Don't make me steal from these people!"

Sikes didn't have the time or the patience for this nonsense. He yanked Oliver to his feet and shook him hard. "I thought I told you to keep quiet," he said. "I warned you what would happen if you didn't do what I said. Now get up and come with me—or else."

Oliver stumbled toward the house, shaking like a leaf in a storm. Sikes led him to a window covered with a wooden shutter. The man pried the shutter open with a crowbar, revealing a tiny window just wide enough for a small boy to crawl through.

"Now you listen to me," Sikes hissed as he handed Oliver a lantern. "I'm going to put you through that window. Take this light and go down the hall to the front door. Then unlock it and let me in. No funny business, hear me?"

"Yes," Oliver whispered. He knew Sikes would kill him if he tried to get away. Sikes pushed him up and through the tiny window, and Oliver landed with a soft thump on the floor.

Courage and determination welled up in Oliver's heart. "I must warn the people here," he said to himself. "I don't care what Sikes does to me! Even if he kills me, it will be better than being a criminal!" He tiptoed down the hallway, intending to run upstairs and warn the family. **Go, Oliver! What a brave boy!** But before Oliver could open his mouth, a light appeared at the end of the hall. Two servants rushed forward, shouting and waving pistols. A shot rang out, and pain tore through Oliver's arm.

Terrified, Oliver bolted back toward the window. Sikes reached down and grabbed him, yanking him up and out.

Oliver was dimly aware of Sikes running and carrying him over one shoulder. Then he felt himself being thrown to the ground and pushed into a ditch. The pain in his arm became unbearable. Darkness swept over him, and he saw and heard no more.

Oh, no! Oliver's been shot, and now it looks like Sikes has abandoned him. Could things possibly get any worse for our hero?

13
A Mysterious Meeting

As you might expect, Fagin is not very happy when he hears that the robbery was unsuccessful. He's even angrier when he finds out that Sikes dumped Oliver in a ditch and left him there to die. What will Fagin do next? Read on!

U pset and distracted, Fagin roamed the streets of London. There was a man he urgently needed to speak to, but he could not find him in any of the usual places. Fagin left word with everyone that he needed to speak to the man called Monks, a mysterious figure who was well-known to the criminal elements of London. After searching all night, he hurried home.

He had just reached the front door of his narrow,

run-down house when a dark figure stepped forward. "Fagin!" the man whispered.

Fagin jumped. "Monks! Is that you?"

"Yes," the man replied. He was a tall, thin man with a wild, nervous look in his eyes. "I have been waiting here for two hours. Where have you been?"

"Looking for you," Fagin replied. "Come inside. I have a great deal to tell you—and none of it is good."

The two men slipped inside. Fagin lit a candle in the kitchen and led his guest to one of the upstairs rooms. "We can talk in here," Fagin assured Monks. "The boys are asleep, and no one will hear us." He placed the candle outside the door.

As Fagin told his guest about the failed robbery in Chertsey, Monks grew angrier and angrier. "It was badly planned!" Monks exclaimed when Fagin had finished. "Why didn't you keep the boy here and make a pickpocket out of him?"

"I saw it was not easy to train him to our business," Fagin explained. "Other boys are quick to take to the criminal life, but Oliver is not like other boys. I needed something to hold over his head to make sure he stayed on our side. If you can't frighten these lads from the start, you have no control over them. Look what happened when I sent him out to pick pockets with the Dodger and Charley."

"I had nothing to do with that little disaster," Monks muttered.

"Of course not. But if all that hadn't happened, you would never have found out who Oliver *really* is. If the boy is alive and returned to me, I will make a thief of him, just as you wanted. And if he is dead—"

"It's no fault of mine if he is!" Monks cried. "I don't want his blood on my hands. I told you—wait!" Monks jumped to his feet and looked around in alarm. "What was that?"

"What?"

"I saw a shadow in the hall. Someone is spying on us!"

Fagin and Monks rushed into the hall, but there was no one there. "You're imagining things," Fagin said.

"I swear I saw someone!" Monks insisted, trembling and glancing around in a panic.

Together the two men searched every room of the house, but they found no one. "I guess I *was* imagining things," Monks said at last, laughing nervously. "I don't feel like talking any more tonight. Fagin, you know what you must do."

Wow, things are getting really interesting here! Who is Monks, and why does he care so much about Oliver? And was someone really spying on the two men? Who could it have been? There are lots of questions to be answered!

14
Oliver Recovers

When we last saw Oliver, he was lying in a ditch, bleeding and unconscious. I'm worried about what happened to him! Let's go back to Chertsey and see what's going on.

Night passed and morning came. A steady rain was falling when Oliver finally woke. He sat up, feeling weak and sick. His arm throbbed, and his sleeve was wet with blood.

Oliver crawled out of the ditch and dragged himself to his feet. He knew that he must find help or he would die. He stumbled along the road, clutching his wounded arm.

The boy looked up and saw a house nearby. "I must go there for help," he said to himself. "Perhaps they will take pity on me. Even if they don't, at least I will not die alone and abandoned!"

But when Oliver finally dragged himself up the

steps of the house, he stopped in fear. This was the very house he had broken into the night before! He stepped back, ready to run away, but he knew he would not get far. So he knocked weakly on the door. Then his strength failed him, and he slid down to sit on the steps.

The door opened and Oliver looked up into several curious faces. "Why, it's just a boy!" the butler of the house exclaimed. "And he's hurt—look at the blood! Quick, bring him inside."

Two men carried Oliver inside while one of the maids ran to tell the owner of the house what had happened. Soon a beautiful girl of about seventeen came downstairs.

"I think it's one of the robbers from last night, Miss Rose," said the butler. "He's shot in one arm."

"Poor fellow! Treat him kindly, for my sake," said the girl. She saw to it that Oliver was put to bed and sent a servant to fetch the doctor. Questions about who Oliver was and how he came to be there would have to wait.

• • • • • •

The owner of the house where Oliver had fled was an elderly woman named Mrs. Maylie. She lived there with her niece, Rose, and several servants. Mrs. Maylie and Rose were very kind and gentle, and they treated Oliver well as he recovered from his wound.

Oliver was very ill, but in time he became strong enough to tell the Maylies the story of how he'd come to be there. It was sad to hear the sick boy's tale of the many terrible things that had happened to him.

Mrs. Maylie and Rose swore that they would do everything in their power to protect and care for Oliver. Seeing him recover under their care was a great reward for the Maylies.

Oliver felt like a changed boy as he basked in the warmth of the Maylies' love. The boy slept well, feeling secure and protected for the first time in many weeks.

The Maylies also owned a beautiful house in the country. When Oliver was well enough, the whole family went to spend several months there. I can tell you, the country is a great place to

be—plenty of room to run, lots of places to dig and hide, and no need to be on a leash all of the time! The country is a great place for a boy too, and Oliver loved it there. But Oliver's past is about to interrupt his happy life once more.

One warm spring day, Oliver was reading in his room. The sun poured in through the window, making him sleepy, and he soon lay his head down on the desk for a short nap.

Suddenly, Oliver felt someone staring at him. He looked up and saw two men standing outside the window. One was tall and thin, with a nervous look on his face. The other man was Fagin!

Oliver struggled to wake up completely. "Yes, that's him, sure enough," he heard Fagin say. Then the two men turned and disappeared.

Oliver blinked and sat up. Fagin had been at the window and had recognized him—he was certain of it! "Rose! Mrs. Maylie!" he shouted, running out of the room. "Help! Fagin is after me!"

Everyone in the house hurried outside to search for the two men. Some of the servants walked over every inch of the property, while others ran down the road, seeking to find the intruders. But no trace of anyone could be found.

"You must have dreamed it, Oliver," said the butler. "Don't worry. You're safe here."

But Oliver was not so sure.

I'm not so sure either. Oliver is definitely in danger! Can anyone help him?

15
A Message from Nancy

So it seems that Fagin is on Oliver's trail again. But Oliver is about to receive some help—from an unexpected source.

"I need money," Bill Sikes muttered to Nancy one evening. "I haven't been able to work since that business at Chertsey, and I haven't sixpence to buy any food or drink! Where's Fagin been these past weeks? I haven't been feeling well, and he hasn't come to see me—not once!"

"Here I am now!" Fagin called cheerfully, sticking his head into the room. The Artful Dodger and Charley Bates entered the room behind him. The Dodger laid a tasty meat pie on the table, while Charley pulled a bottle from one of his coat pockets.

Bull's-eye crawled out from under the bed as soon as his nose caught a whiff of the meat pie. He began to dance around the table, jumping up and down in an attempt to reach the food.

"I've never seen such a jolly dog," Charley Bates said, laughing. "He'd make a fortune on the stage, he would, dancing so funny."

"Get down, you!" Sikes shouted at the dog. Bull's-eye slunk back under the bed, growling.

"Eat up, Bill," Fagin said. "I heard you were sick, so I've brought you some vittles."

"That's right, I haven't been feeling well," Sikes grumbled. "I might have died twenty times over before you came to help me. Where have you been?"

"I was away from London for a time, tending to business," Fagin said. "But I didn't forget about you, Bill."

"I'll bet," Sikes muttered darkly.

"Oh, leave the old man alone, Bill," Nancy said. "He said he didn't forget about you, and he brought you a lovely meal. Can't you leave it at that?"

"No, I can't," Sikes replied. "I need some money, Fagin. It's been weeks since I've been able to do a job."

"I haven't a single coin on me," Fagin said.

"You've got lots at home," Sikes shot back. "I need some money tonight, and that's that."

"All right," said Fagin with a loud sigh. "I'll send the Dodger around to fetch it."

"Oh, no, you won't. I know that lad—he'll forget to come back or lose his way, or some such excuse. Nancy shall go back with you and bring the money here."

So it was decided. Nancy, Fagin, and the boys walked back to Fagin's house. "Dodger, Charley, you go to work now," Fagin told them. "It's nearly ten o'clock, and you haven't done anything useful all day."

The boys ran off. Fagin was just about to give Nancy the money when he heard footsteps in the hall. Fagin peered out, then quickly ducked back into the room.

"Nancy, there's a man here to see me. You just sit tight. This won't take a moment."

Nancy nodded and sat at the table until Fagin was out of the room. Nancy was curious. Who was Fagin talking to and what was it about? She slipped off her shoes and tiptoed into the hall, determined to listen to their conversation.

Fifteen minutes later, Nancy slipped back into the room as quietly as she had left it. The words she had overheard left her pale and trembling. The men had found Oliver with a wealthy family called the Maylies. Oliver was in terrible danger!

"Why, Nancy, how pale you are," Fagin said when he returned, looking at her closely. "Are you sick?"

"Am I pale?" Nancy said rather wildly. She put a hand to her cheek.

"Yes, you look quite horrible. What have you been doing?"

"Nothing! It's just sitting in this stuffy room, I suppose. Let me have the money and I'll be off."

Fagin did as she asked, and Nancy hurried outside. As soon as she turned the corner, she burst into tears and began to run as if some horrible monster was chasing her. Nancy decided that the danger to herself did not matter. She had to help Oliver.

"I mustn't let Bill see me like this!" Nancy said to herself. She wiped her eyes and took a deep breath, then headed up to Sikes's room.

"Did you get the money?" Sikes growled from the bed.

"Yes."

"Good. Bring me a drink. There's a good girl."

Nancy hurried to do as he asked. Sikes didn't see the powder she slipped into the drink when he wasn't looking. He drained the glass, and in a few moments was fast asleep.

Quickly, Nancy pulled on her bonnet and shawl and hurried outside again. Running through the streets, she came to an elegant hotel in one of the nicest parts of town. "I must speak to Miss Maylie," she told the man at the door. Nancy had overheard Monks—Fagin's earlier visitor—mention Rose's name and say that she was staying in this hotel during a visit to London.

The man looked Nancy up and down as if he did not like what he saw. "What name am I to give her?" he asked stiffly.

"It's of no use to give my name," Nancy replied. "Miss Maylie doesn't know me, but I *must* speak to her."

"Get away from here," the man said, losing his patience.

"No! You'll have to carry me out," Nancy threatened, "and I'll make sure it won't be easy. Isn't there anyone here who will carry a simple message for a poor girl like me?" She was determined to help Oliver. She couldn't let that poor, sweet boy come to a bad end!

The cook came out of the kitchen in time to hear Nancy's desperate plea. "Go on," he said to the doorman. "What harm will it do to bring Miss Maylie the message?"

The doorman laughed. "You don't think Miss Maylie will see her, do you?"

"That's for Miss Maylie to decide," the cook said.

"Oh, all right," the doorman said and headed upstairs. He returned a few minutes later and motioned Nancy to follow him. "Miss Maylie will see you in her room," he said.

"Sit down," said Rose when Nancy entered the room. "Who are you and what do you have to tell me?"

"There is a boy staying with you named Oliver Twist, am I right?" Nancy asked.

Rose sat up in surprise. "Why, yes. Do you know him?"

"I am the girl who dragged him back to Fagin's on the night he ran an errand for the gentleman at Pentonville. I am a member of that gang which held Oliver prisoner. But I have slipped away from them tonight to tell you something I overheard. If they knew I was here, they would murder me for sure!"

Rose leaned forward. "Oh, you poor girl!" she cried. "Tell me everything."

"Do you know a man named Monks?" Nancy asked her. Rose shook her head no. "Well, he knows you," Nancy continued. "And he knows Oliver—in fact, he has been looking for the boy for some time. When he found out Fagin had Oliver, Monks made a bargain with him. He promised a certain sum of money to Fagin if he made the boy into a thief."

"But why?" Rose asked.

"Monks said that he would do anything to ruin Oliver," Nancy said. "Then he said, 'Fagin, you never laid such a trap as I will for my young brother, Oliver.'"

"His brother!"

"Those were his very words." Nancy looked around nervously. "It's getting late, and I must go back before someone misses me."

"Go back?" Rose repeated in astonishment. "Why would you want to go back to such rough company?"

"It is the only life I know," Nancy said sadly, "and those people are the closest thing I have to a family. I have told you all I know. Now it is up to you to save Oliver."

Rose pleaded with Nancy to stay with her, but the girl refused. "All right, leave if you must," Rose said at last. "But where can I find you again if I need to?"

"Every Sunday night from eleven till the clock strikes midnight, I will walk on London Bridge," Nancy promised. "Now I must run. God bless you, Miss Maylie, and thank you!" With those words, Nancy hurried out of the room.

Rose sat, stunned. "I must tell this news to someone—I can't help Oliver on my own," she said. "But who can help me?"

Rose did not get much sleep that night, for her mind was filled with this threat to Oliver. The next morning, as she sat thinking, Oliver himself ran into the room.

"I saw him! I saw him!" the boy shouted, jumping up and down in excitement.

"Saw who?" Rose asked.

"Mr. Brownlow, the gentleman who was so good to me," Oliver said, grinning. "He was getting out of his carriage and going into a house on Craven Street. I'm going to see him now. I can't wait to tell him all that has happened to me. At last I can explain to him why I never returned that night I was kidnapped, and let him know that I am not a thief!"

Suddenly, Rose knew who she should confide in. "I

will go with you," she said, reaching for her hat and coat. "I am very eager to talk to Mr. Brownlow about you."

Five minutes later, Rose and Oliver were on their way. When they arrived at Mr. Brownlow's house, Rose told Oliver to wait and went in by herself. She told Mr. Brownlow's servant that she needed to see him on very important business and was told to go upstairs into the old gentleman's study.

Mr. Brownlow was not alone. His friend, the odd-looking Mr. Grimwig, was also in the room. Rose recognized Mr. Grimwig from Oliver's description of him.

"Thank you for agreeing to see me, sir," Rose said. "I think the news I bring will surprise both of you very much. Mr. Brownlow, you were once very kind to a dear young friend of mine. His name is Oliver Twist."

When Mr. Grimwig heard Oliver's name, he dropped the book he'd been holding and fell back in his chair. He stared in wonder for a long moment, and then jerked himself up with a long, deep whistle.

Mr. Brownlow was no less surprised. He drew his chair close to Rose and said, "I trusted the boy once, but after he disappeared from my house, I was forced to think he was just a thief. If you can change my opinion, please do so at once!"

Rose quickly filled the gentlemen in on all that had happened to Oliver since he had left Mr. Brownlow's house. "His only sorrow these past months has been that you thought he was a thief," she finished.

"You have brought me great happiness," Mr. Brownlow said. "Tell me, where is the boy now? Why didn't you bring him with you?"

"He is waiting in the carriage outside," Rose said.

Mr. Brownlow jumped to his feet and hurried outside. Shortly he came back into the room with Oliver. It was difficult to tell who was more excited.

"There is somebody else who should not be forgotten," Mr. Brownlow said, ringing for a servant. "Send Mrs. Bedwin here, please," he ordered.

The old housekeeper hurried into the room and waited for Mr. Brownlow to tell her what he wanted.

"Put on your glasses, Mrs. Bedwin," Mr. Brownlow said, "and see if you can't figure out why I called you here."

Mrs. Bedwin began to fumble in her pocket for

her glasses, but Oliver could wait no longer. He ran into her arms.

"It's my innocent boy!" the housekeeper cried, hugging Oliver tightly. "I knew you would come back. I thought of you every day. Every day!" The old lady ran her fingers fondly through Oliver's hair, laughing and crying at the same time.

While this happy reunion was going on, Mr. Brownlow led Rose into another room. Rose told him everything Nancy had spoken of regarding the man named Monks and his plot against Oliver.

"We must find this man, Monks, and get him to confess," Mr. Brownlow said. "It is the only way to get to the bottom of the mystery of who Oliver really is. On Sunday night, you and I will go to London Bridge to meet with Nancy."

With Rose and Mr. Brownlow working together, they're sure to sniff out some clues to who Monks is and why he is so interested in Oliver. But can they stop him before he gets Oliver into his clutches? Read on, and you'll see!

16
Suspicion

After her meeting with Rose Maylie,
Nancy spends a long, nervous week
waiting for Sunday night to arrive.
At last, the clock strikes eleven,
and Nancy prepares to go out.
But things don't go quite as
she plans.

"What a dark, gloomy night this is," Sikes
said to Fagin. "It would be a good night
for business."

"Yes," Fagin agreed. "What a pity we don't have anything planned for tonight."

"You're right for once," replied Sikes gruffly.

Fagin was about to reply when he noticed Nancy putting on her bonnet. He gestured to Sikes and raised his eyebrows.

"Hey, Nancy, where do you think you're going at this time of night?" Sikes asked.

"Not far," the girl replied, heading for the door.

"I asked you where," Sikes said threateningly.

"I don't know where," Nancy said.

"Well, I do," said Sikes. "Nowhere! Sit down."

"Oh, Bill, don't be this way," Nancy begged. "I just want to get a breath of fresh air."

"Stick your head out the window then," Sikes said. Without another word, he locked the door, pocketed the key, and pulled Nancy's bonnet off. "You're not going anywhere."

"Bill, please let me go out," Nancy said. Sikes just glared at her. "Fagin, tell him to let me go," Nancy said, turning to the old man for help. "It would only be for an hour. Please!"

"I said no!" Sikes roared. He pushed the girl roughly into another room and sat watching her to make sure she could not escape.

Nancy begged and screamed for an hour, but Sikes would not change his mind. Finally, when the clock struck midnight, Nancy fell silent. Shaking his head, Sikes went back to join Fagin at the table.

"I don't know what's gotten into her," Sikes complained. "She's never been this way before."

"You're right," said Fagin. "I've never seen her get so upset over such a small matter."

Nancy came into the room and sat quietly in the corner. Her eyes were red from crying. Fagin stared at her thoughtfully for a few minutes, and then got up to leave. "Can someone light my way down the stairs?" the old man asked.

"Go on, Nancy, light his way," Sikes grumbled. "We wouldn't want our friend to break his neck, now would we?"

Nancy lit a candle and followed Fagin down the narrow staircase. When they reached the bottom, Fagin leaned close to her and whispered, "What is it, Nancy, my dear?"

"What do you mean?" Nancy said carefully.

"Do you want to leave Bill?" Fagin asked. "Is that the reason for the fuss you made tonight?"

"No!" Nancy cried sharply, backing away.

"All right," Fagin soothed her. "We'll talk about it some other time. Don't forget, I'm your friend, Nancy. If you want help, you only have to come to me."

Nancy shook her head. "Good night," she said and hurried back upstairs.

Fagin walked toward his own home, thinking hard about all that had happened that evening. "Nancy must be tired of Bill," he said to himself. "Maybe she has a new boyfriend, but she knows Bill would never let her leave." He thought further. "I wouldn't mind taking Bill out of the picture. He knows things that could get me in trouble with the police, and I don't trust him to keep his mouth shut. Maybe Nancy would be willing to help me get rid of him. How can I convince her?"

Fagin pondered how to make everything turn out the way he'd like. "I know what to do," he said at last. "I'll have someone follow her and find out who her new boyfriend is. Then I'll threaten to reveal the whole story to Bill. She'll do anything I ask to prevent that from happening. What power I'll have over her! She'll have to do anything I ask—anything!" The old man clenched his fingers together, twisting them tightly, as though Bill Sikes's neck was in their grasp.

What a rotten guy this Fagin is! He wants to get rid of his partner, but he wants Nancy to do all the dirty work and take the blame. What will happen when he finds out that Nancy doesn't have a new boyfriend, and that saving Oliver is what she's really up to? I think things are about to get very interesting in old London town.

17
Betrayed!

The following Sunday night, Nancy is able to slip away from Bill Sikes. As she heads for London Bridge, she doesn't know that someone is following her, ready to report everything that happens to Fagin.

The church clocks chimed three quarters past eleven as two figures stepped onto London Bridge. One was Nancy, who looked anxiously about her as she walked. The other figure was a young man who slunk along in the shadows a few steps behind her, careful not to be seen.

Nancy stopped at the center of the bridge and leaned against the rail. The bridge was almost deserted that dark, misty night, and the few people who passed the girl paid no attention to her.

Just as the clock struck twelve, Rose Maylie and Mr. Brownlow stepped out of a carriage and walked onto the bridge. Nancy hurried to meet them. "I'm afraid to speak to you here in the open," Nancy whispered. "Let's go down these steps to someplace more private."

The three made their way down the stairs that led to a landing by the river. The spy also moved over there, slipping unseen behind a corner of the wall. From this spot, he could hear every word that Nancy and her companions said.

"Where were you last Sunday night?" Mr.

Brownlow asked. "We waited for you on the bridge, but you did not come."

"I couldn't come," Nancy replied. "They wouldn't let me out."

"Do your companions suspect anything?" Mr. Brownlow asked, looking around.

"No," Nancy answered. "They don't suspect a thing. The man who kept me in last Sunday is sleeping now, thanks to a powder I slipped in his drink."

"Good," Mr. Brownlow said. "Rose has told me everything you said regarding this man called Monks. Can you describe Monks to me and tell me where I might find him?"

"Yes, but first you must promise never to tell Monks that I spoke to you," Nancy insisted. "My companions must never know my part in this. If they ever found out, my life would be in great danger."

"You have our word," Mr. Brownlow said.

"Good. Now then, Monks is a tall, dark man. He is very nervous, and he often looks over his shoulder as he walks, as if checking for spies. And he has a scar on his neck—"

"A scar?" Mr. Brownlow interrupted her. "Is it a thick red line just above his collar?"

"Why, yes," Nancy replied. "Do you know him?"

"Possibly. If it's the man I'm thinking of, why—" Mr. Brownlow took a deep breath. "Never mind. Go on."

Nancy went on to tell Mr. Brownlow the location of a public house where Monks could be found. "You have given us very valuable information," Mr. Brownlow said when Nancy had finished. "What can I do to help you?"

"Nothing," Nancy said. "I am past all help."

"If you come with me, I can keep you safe from these companions of yours," Mr. Brownlow said. "I will find a place for you far from London, where they will never find you. Tell us the names of these wicked friends of yours, and I will see that they are brought to justice. Then you will truly be safe."

Nancy shook her head. "I cannot leave my life, as much as I would like to. It is too late for me to turn back now. And I cannot turn against my companions. All I ask is that you help Oliver. I must go." With that, Nancy turned and ran up the stairs, disappearing into the gloom.

After Rose and Mr. Brownlow had left, the spy stepped out of the shadows and hurried away toward Fagin's house to report all he had heard.

As you can imagine, Fagin is furious when he hears what Nancy is up to. He doesn't waste any time in sending word to Bill Sikes, telling him to come for an emergency meeting right away.

Fagin crouched over the fireplace, lost in thought. All his plans to get rid of Bill Sikes were ruined! And if Brownlow got hold of Monks, Monks might tell him everything he knew about Fagin. His whole life would be ruined! How dare Nancy betray the gang to strangers!

Fagin's anger grew stronger and stronger. Finally, he heard a footstep in the hall. "At last!" he muttered as Bill Sikes strode into the room.

"What's going on?" Sikes asked, sitting down at the table. He drew back at the sight of Fagin's grim face. "You look like you could kill somebody."

"I've something to tell you, Bill," Fagin said. "When you hear it, you'll be even angrier than I am."

"Go ahead," Sikes said, leaning forward. "Say what you've got to say."

"Suppose some member of our gang was to meet with a gentleman and tell him our business. Suppose this person was to sneak out at night and tell this gentleman things that could land all of us in jail. What would you do?"

"What would I do?" Sikes repeated. "Why, I'd grind his skull under my boot into as many grains as there are hairs on his head!"

"What if *I* did it?" Fagin asked.

"I'd do the same."

"What if it were Charley or the Dodger or—"

"I don't care who it was," Sikes replied. "Whoever it was, I'd do my worst to him."

Fagin looked hard at the thief. Then he whispered, "What if it was Nancy? What if Nancy went to London Bridge and met two people who asked her to give up all of her pals? What if she betrayed us to them? What if she described our friend Monks to them so they could find him and question him, and told him exactly where Monks could be found? And what if she said that she had gotten away from you by putting a sleeping powder in your drink, so you would not keep her from meeting with them? What would you do then?"

Sikes shoved himself to his feet. He was trembling with rage. "Let me out of here," he roared. "Don't say another word!"

"Bill, you won't be too violent, will you?" Fagin asked.

Day was just breaking, and there was enough light for the men to see each other's faces. They exchanged one brief glance, and there was a fire in the eyes of both that could not be mistaken. Then Sikes wrenched open the door and ran into the street.

Sikes walked straight home, staring ahead with savage determination. He went into his room and locked the door. Nancy was asleep on her bed.

"Get up!" Sikes shouted at her.

Nancy rose and began to pull back the curtain, for the room was dim in the early morning light.

"Let it be," Sikes said, pushing her hand away from the window. "There's light enough for what I've got to do."

Nancy stared at him nervously. "Bill," she asked in a shaking voice, "why are you looking at me like that? What have I done?"

"You know what you have done, and so do I,"

Sikes told her. "You were followed tonight, and every word you said was overheard and reported to Fagin and me."

"Bill, don't hurt me," Nancy begged. "I have been true to you. I didn't tell them anything about you. Let's run away together, just you and me. We can lead better lives, I know we can!"

Sikes would not listen to another word. He raised his hand and struck Nancy hard, over and over again, until the girl fell to the floor.

Sikes stepped back in horror. "What have I done?" he cried. He whistled for his dog to follow him, then stumbled out of the house, away from the terrible murder he had committed.

Poor Nancy! She was only trying to do what was right, and she paid with her life. Will her sacrifice help Oliver? Read on!

18
The Truth Is Revealed

Nancy's body is soon discovered, and all of London is outraged by the crime. Bill Sikes is on the run, but there's nowhere to hide— everyone is combing the city to find him. Meanwhile, let's check in with Mr. Brownlow and see if he's found the mysterious Monks yet.

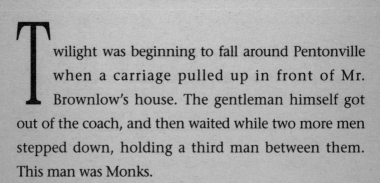

T wilight was beginning to fall around Pentonville when a carriage pulled up in front of Mr. Brownlow's house. The gentleman himself got out of the coach, and then waited while two more men stepped down, holding a third man between them. This man was Monks.

The men followed Mr. Brownlow into a back room of the house. "You know what to do," Mr. Brownlow told the men. "If Monks tries to leave this room or does anything to harm me, call for the police."

"By what authority am I kidnapped in the street and brought here?" Monks demanded.

"By mine," Mr. Brownlow replied, steel in his voice. "If you do not do as I ask, I have enough evidence against you to have you arrested on charges of fraud and robbery. I don't think the police will be very kind to you."

Monks hesitated, muttering to himself. "Is there no other way?" he asked at last.

"None," was Mr. Brownlow's firm reply.

"All right, then," Monks said. "I will do as you ask." He threw his hat and cloak down and scowled at Mr. Brownlow. "This is fine treatment from my father's oldest friend."

"It is because I was his friend that I am treating you as kindly as I am," Mr. Brownlow replied. "Listen well. You have a brother. You gave yourself away when I whispered his name in your ear on the street today."

"I have no brother," Monks insisted.

"You're lying. Your real name is Edward Leeford," Mr. Brownlow stated. "Your father was Edwin Leeford.

When he was young, his family forced him into an unhappy marriage. You are the child of that ill-fated union."

"Yes," Monks admitted. "That much is true."

"In time, the marriage failed completely, and your parents separated," Mr. Brownlow went on. "Your father fell in love with a young girl named Agnes."

"Yes, yes," Monks said in a bored voice. "What has any of this to do with me?"

"Before Agnes and your father could marry, he was called to Rome on business. While there, he caught a fever and died suddenly. He had stopped to see me on his way to Rome, and he left several items in my possession. One was a painting of Agnes, which hangs downstairs. When Oliver was recovering from illness here, his strong resemblance to that portrait struck me like a thunderbolt. You see, Agnes was expecting a baby when Edwin Leeford traveled to Rome. Oliver—the boy I rescued from the streets—is their son, and your half-brother."

"So what if he is?" Monks shouted. "You think to charge me with some crime based on the resemblance of an orphan boy to a painting of a dead woman? You can't prove anything!"

"I can and I have," Mr. Brownlow said. "Before he died, your father left a will leaving much of his property to Agnes and her unborn child. **A will is a legal document saying who will inherit—receive—a person's money and property after the person dies.** Your mother destroyed that will so she could keep Edwin's wealth for herself—and for you. You spent your life trying to locate Oliver. When you finally discovered him in Fagin's clutches, you conspired with that villain to trap the boy in a life of poverty and crime so you would never have to give the child the inheritance that was properly his!"

"No!" cried Monks, overwhelmed by these charges.

"Yes," Mr. Brownlow said firmly. "Every word that passed between you and Fagin was overheard and reported to me. The poor girl who told me was murdered because of her honesty. You are an accomplice to that murder, for it was your deceit that caused all of this to happen."

"No!" Monks shouted. "I had nothing to do with murder!"

"Will you swear that all I have said concerning your brother's inheritance and your father's missing will are true?" Mr. Brownlow asked. "If you do, I will not connect you to Nancy's murder."

Monks began to pace up and down, debating with himself whether he could do as Mr. Brownlow demanded. "I will do what you ask," Monks said reluctantly.

"You will do more than that," Mr. Brownlow pressed on. "You will pay Oliver his share of the inheritance."

Just then, a friend of Mr. Brownlow's knocked on the door and hurried into the room. "The murderer, Sikes, is sure to be captured tonight!" he said. "We've seen his dog, which means he has returned to one of his hideouts. The police are on his trail!"

Mr. Brownlow turned to Monks. "You see there is no escape," he said. "Have you made up your mind?"

"Yes," Monks said, knowing he was trapped. "I will do all that you ask."

"I will draw up a legal document outlining the

terms of our agreement," Mr. Brownlow said. "You will remain here until it is ready to be signed. This is the safest place for you now."

Monks agreed, and Mr. Brownlow left the room, locking the door behind him.

So Oliver and Monks really are brothers! What a low-down dirty trick to cheat Oliver out of what rightfully belongs to him. Three cheers for Mr. Brownlow for making sure justice is done! But what about Bill Sikes? Will he receive justice for Nancy's murder? We're about to find out!

19
The End of Sikes

Along the Thames there was a strange, polluted neighborhood called Jacob's Island. This small collection of run-down houses and abandoned warehouses was surrounded by a creek about six or eight feet deep called Folly Ditch. Sometimes, when the tide ran high, the ditch filled with water and the neighborhood truly was an island. But most of the time, Folly Ditch was little more than a muddy swamp, adding a damp, dismal air to the dreary neighborhood.

Thames is the name of the river that runs through London. It's pronounced TEMZ.

The houses on Jacob's Island had no owners—they had all been abandoned. People who had nowhere else to go had broken into these shabby buildings, and here they scratched out a miserable life.

Several members of Fagin's gang were gathered in an upper room of one of these abandoned houses. "All of London is up in arms over Nancy's murder," one of the thieves said. "The crowds will do anything to see Bill Sikes punished. Even Fagin's been captured!"

"I know. I was there," another man said. "Charley Bates and I barely escaped when the police broke in. Fagin and everyone else in the room were arrested on the spot."

"They say Fagin will hang for all his crimes," the first thief said.

"That's right. There will be quite a crowd at that execution!" **In those days, criminals were hung in public, and large crowds gathered to watch.**

Just then there was a noise on the stairs. Bull's-eye bounded into the room.

"What is the meaning of this?" one of the thieves yelled. "That's Sikes's dog! Wherever Bull's-eye is, Sikes can't be far behind. Don't tell me he's coming *here*!"

Suddenly there was a knock at the door below. "Is that Charley Bates?" one of the men asked.

"No, he never knocks like that," the second thief

answered. He walked over to the window and peered outside. "It's Sikes!" he cried in horror. At the sound of his master's name, the dog jumped to his feet and ran, whining, to the door.

"We must let him in," the first man replied. "I'll go down and open the door for him."

When the thief returned, Sikes was with him, a kerchief wrapped over his head to hide his face. Sikes pulled the kerchief off, revealing a pale face, sunken cheeks, and wild eyes. He looked like a ghost.

Silence lay heavy in the dim room. "Have you nothing to say to me?" Sikes asked at last.

The others shook their heads in fear.

"Can I stay here until the hunt is over?"

"If you must," one of the thieves replied.

Another knock came at the door and Sikes jumped. "Who's that?" he growled.

"That's Charley's knock," the thief replied. He went down to let the boy in.

When Charley walked in and saw Sikes, he stopped suddenly. "What are you doing here?" he asked.

"Charley, it's me, your old pal Sikes," the man said, taking a step toward the boy.

"Don't come near me, you monster! Anyone who could kill Nancy is no pal of mine!" Charley screamed. He ran to the window, leaned out, and began to shout, "Help! The murderer is here! Help!"

Lights gleamed in the street below, and footsteps hurried toward the house. "Break down the door! Help!" Charley screamed as Sikes lunged toward him and wrestled him to the floor.

"Be quiet!" the murderer hissed. He dragged the still-yelling Charley into another room and locked him in. But it was too late for Sikes. Heavy blows rained down on the door below, and a crowd of people shouted for Sikes to come out.

"I'll beat you yet!" Sikes roared down to the crowd. "Give me a long rope," he demanded of his companions. "The crowd is at the front of the house. I can go around to the back, drop into Folly Ditch, and clear out that way. Hurry! Give me a rope, or I'll kill you too."

The panic-stricken thieves hurried to do as Sikes asked. Sikes ran to the roof and looked out over the edge to the muddy ditch below.

"He's gone around to the back!" Charley Bates

shouted down to the crowd through the window of the room where Sikes had locked him. "Hurry!"

Sikes crouched on the roof and watched the crowd surge around the house. Escape seemed impossible, but he knew he had to try. He tied a loop in the rope and slipped it over his head. He was just about to pull it under his arms when he lost his balance and tumbled over the edge. The rope tightened around his neck as he fell, and his body swung heavily against the house.

Charley watched everything from the window of his prison. "He's dead," he shouted down to the crowd. "Now get me out of here!"

How brave Charley was to turn against Sikes the way he did! Even though he was angry and scared, Charley knew that giving Sikes up was the right thing to do. Now it's time to turn our attention back to Oliver. What's happened to our young hero? The next chapter will tell us everything.

20
Finally Home

Two days after Sikes's death, Oliver found himself seated in a carriage, traveling to the town where he was born. Mrs. Maylie, Rose, and Mrs. Bedwin were with him. Mr. Brownlow followed them in another carriage, along with a man Oliver had not yet met.

The carriages stopped in front of the town's best hotel. Mr. Brownlow's friend, Mr. Grimwig, was there to greet them. He seemed very glad to see Oliver, and never once mentioned that day when he and Mr. Brownlow had waited in vain for Oliver to return.

It was nine o'clock that night when everyone gathered in an upstairs room. Mr. Grimwig and Mr. Brownlow were the last to enter. Between them walked a nervous-looking man who Mr. Brownlow introduced as Oliver's brother—Edward Leeford, who called himself Monks.

"Why, that is the man who was with Fagin,

spying on me through the window," Oliver said in surprise.

Monks gave Oliver a look filled with hatred.

Mr. Brownlow stepped forward and laid a hand on Oliver's head. "This is your half-brother," he said to Monks, "the son of your father and poor Agnes Fleming."

"Yes," Monks said without emotion. "That is their child."

"Edwin died in Rome before Oliver was born. Now, Monks, when you and your mother went to Rome after your father died, what did you find?"

"We looked through his papers and found a will," Monks admitted. "It said the bulk of his property was to go to Agnes and her unborn child. My mother burned the will so that Father's fortune would pass entirely to us."

"When you found out that Oliver was your half-brother, you asked Fagin to trap the boy into a life of crime so that he could never claim his rightful inheritance, did you not?" Mr. Brownlow asked.

"I did," Monks said.

"I have drawn up legal papers stating all of the

above," Mr. Brownlow said. "Monks will sign them, and we will see that Oliver receives his rightful share of the inheritance."

Monks grudgingly agreed and the papers were signed. Oliver was now a wealthy little boy. His real wealth, however, could not be measured in gold. It was the treasure of love and caring from his devoted friends.

Oliver's fortune was not just money. He now had many people who loved and cared for him too. Here's what happened to Oliver after he received his inheritance.

The provisions of his father's will entitled Oliver to all of Monks's fortune—a vast amount of money. But kind-hearted Mr. Brownlow suggested that Oliver be generous and give a fair portion to Monks. Monks took his share and moved to the United States, where he spent his money foolishly and died in poverty.

As for Fagin, he was arrested and charged for his connection to Nancy's murder, and for all his other crimes too. The old thief was hung in front of a cheering crowd.

Oliver fared much better. Mr. Brownlow adopted him as his son and saw that he had everything any boy could want. The little family moved out to the country to live near the Maylies. Here Oliver, surrounded by the love of his adopted father and his very good friends, lived happily ever after.

What a great story! Oliver finally got all the good things in life—including a full supper dish. Now if only my food bowl were full—hey! Look at that! I was so busy reading OLIVER TWIST with you that I didn't even notice someone filled up my dish. See ya later—I've got some serious eating to do!

A little dog with a big imagination!^{SM}

Let television's canine hero be your tour guide...

and don't miss any of the WISHBONE™ retellings of these classic adventures!

WISHBONE™

OLIVER TWIST • Charles Dickens
DON QUIXOTE • Miguel de Cervantes
ROMEO & JULIET • William Shakespeare
JOAN OF ARC • Mark Twain
THE ODYSSEY • Homer

Each WISHBONE™ book only $3.99!

And coming soon...

THE ADVENTURES OF ROBIN HOOD
FRANKENSTEIN • Mary Shelley
THE STRANGE CASE OF DR. JEKYLL AND MR. HYDE
• Robert Louis Stevenson

MAIL TO: **HarperCollins Publishers,**
P.O. Box 588 Dunmore, PA 18512-0588
Yes, please send me the WISHBONE™ Classics I have checked:

**Visa & MasterCard holders
call 1-800-331-3761**

❏ *The Odyssey* by Homer, retold by Joanne Mattern 106413-0 ....$3.99 U.S./ $4.99 Can.
❏ *Don Quixote* by Miguel de Cervantes, retold by Michael Burgan 106416-5 ....$3.99 U.S./ $4.99 Can.
❏ *Romeo & Juliet* by William Shakespeare, retold by William Aronson 106415-7 ....$3.99 U.S./ $4.99 Can.
❏ *Joan of Arc* by Mark Twain, retold by Patrice Selene 106418-1 ....$3.99 U.S./ $4.99 Can.
❏ *Oliver Twist* by Charles Dickens, retold by Joanne Mattern 106419-X ....$3.99 U.S./ $4.99 Can.

Name _____
Address _____
City _____ State _____ Zip _____

SUBTOTAL ....$_____
POSTAGE & HANDLING .$_____
SALES TAX ....$_____
(Add applicable sales tax)
TOTAL ....$_____

Order 4 or more titles and postage & handling is FREE! For orders of less than 4 books, please
____ ___ postage & handling. Allow up to 6 weeks for delivery. Remit in U.S. funds.
____ ___ U.S. & Canada. Prices subject to change. H155